Winter Birds Of Christmas

Copyright © 2020

Written by Beth Roose
Illustrated by Elaine Maier

First Edition 2020

# Dedication

This book is dedicated to my granddaughter. Sophia may you always know the spirit of Christmas and how to follow after your dreams. And to my Son Mathew and his wonderful wife Liz may you always know love and happiness.

*Winter Birds of Christmas*

Elf Sophia had been out in the pine trees, gathering nuts and berries. Elf Sophia was so thankful she had the help of Santa's winter birds to collect nuts and berries.

Out of the corner of her eyes, Elf Sophia saw something move. She looked more closely at the big pine tree. Sure enough, underneath the big pine branch near the ground, was a small squirrel.

tacy flew down to greet the small squirrel. The small squirrel was pointing to a large pile of what looked like acorns. Soon Elf Sophia was kneeling in the snow beside Stacy and the small squirrel.

All three looked at the large pile of acorns. There was a beautiful red ribbon tied around each acorn! The small squirrel hopped over to the pile of acorns. Just then the other winter birds flew down and joined the group. The small squirrel said he had worked very hard this Christmas season gathering the acorns and wrapping red ribbons around each one.

All six of Santa's winter birds watched as Elf Sophia pulled glittering Elf Dust out of her gold pouch.

Elf Sophia blew on the glittering Elf Dust. The Elf Dust began to sparkle as it floated down and covered the acorns. The sparkle soon disappeared.

Just then Santa appeared. Santa greeted
the little squirrel with a wink and smile.

The little squirrel had been gathering the acorns as gifts for all small creatures of the woodlands. Even in the woodlands, Elf Sophia could see the spirit of Christmas.

Elf Sophia knew that, by adding the
glittering Elf Dust, the magic of Christmas
would be alive for all creatures, big or small.

Santa, Elf Sophia, and the winter birds helped deliver Christmas acorns that day. The winter birds looked so pretty as they flew about carrying the acorns with the beautiful red ribbons tied around them."

Santa exclaimed, "Christmas is alive for all who believe, including the creatures, big and small, living in the woodlands."

# About the Author

We are commited to inspire children of all ages. We produce animated films, films, music video's, and host CinaMagic Classic Films. Beth Roose Films takes a "flash" forward approach to digital animation, combining technology with experience as well as cutting edge design "flying" animation into the next generation.

Our goal is to produce animated films, television series, books, interactive content and visual effects. Beth Roose Film is aggressively pursuing this goal by developing original content and working toward developing strategic alliances with other independents in order to collaborate with them on exciting and creative projects.

Beth Roose plays an important part in bringing animated cartoon with a moral and family oriented message to children of all ages. Drawing on universal themes, like good versus evil and family, the films featured songs, humor, slapstick, and emotion, all with intricate scenery, detailed drawing, and wonderful musical scores.

Our animated films "Elf Sparkle Meets Christmas The Horse" and "Jimmy Paul The Pug Tooth Fairy" both hold the "Dove" seal for family programming. In addition, both films have won many film festivals.

# Books By Beth Roose

## Funny Elmer

Funny Elmer will make you laugh as he goes about his life on the farm. Elmer thinks he is the family dog and also discovers he likes to skate on the frozen pond. However, what Elmer likes most will make you laugh out loud.

## Elf Sparkle And The Special Red Dress

Did you know elves receive special gifts from Santa? Elf Figgy Puddin wrote a special letter to Santa asking that he grant Elf Sparkle the very first Christmas gift of the Christmas Season.

## Everett Covered Bridge

A little Boy and his beloved dog Curtis makes friends with a Great Blue Heron and her family. They become close friends, but as the winter season approaches they are faced with saying goodbye to each other.

## Elf Sparkle Meets Christmas The Horse

Families will love the adorable Elf Sparkle as she and Santa go for a test ride on the sleigh but end up in the middle of a rain storm. They must put the sleigh down at Horseshoe Pond in the Cuyahoga Valley National Park. It is there they meet Christmas the Horse.

# Books By Beth Roose

## Grandma Mabel Rescues Pearl

Grandma Mabel Rescues Pearl is a book about helping others in need. Putting others before yourself is sometimes a lesson we learn later in life.

## Santa's Lost Keys

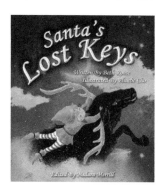

A Magical journey ensues as Elf Magic realizes she lost Santa's keys. She retraces her steps that day which included a trip to Ice Box Cave. It is truly a magical and heartwarming adventure.

## Jimmy Paul The Pug Tooth Fairy

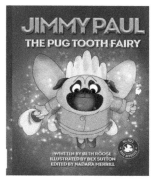

Every child dreams of seeing the tooth fairy... And dogs are no exception. This happy dog family is planning to capture Jimmy Paul The Tooth Fairy... Your whole family will enjoy this family friendly adventure.

## Toodles The Pink Poodle

This Pink Poodle Birthday Party is styled to perfection by the waitstaff! Elva Mae, Toodles, and her pink and white dalmatians friends make it a happy PINK birthday celebration by wearing their pink sunglasses to the Pink Poodle Party.

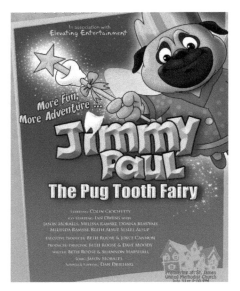

## JIMMY PAUL THE PUG TOOTH FAIRY

Every child dreams of seeing the tooth fairy... And dogs are no exception. This happy dog family is planning to capture Jimmy Paul The Tooth Fairy... Your whole family will enjoy this family friendly adventure.

## ELF SPARKLE MEETS CHRISTMAS THE HORSE

This is a musical animated story that is truly enchanting for both children and adults. Families will love the adorable Elf Sparkle as she and Santa go for a test ride on the sleigh but end up in the middle of a rain storm. They meet Christmas the Horse and with a little help from a dash of elf dust, Christmas is able to pull the sleigh out of the mud and they all head to the North Pole for Christmas.

Dove Worldview:
*Here is a cute animated story for the Christmas season that your children will love year after year. With wonderful music to charm the audience, Sparkle and Santa take them on a toe tapping adventure. This short holiday story will entertain the entire family and you will want to add it to your collection of Christmas DVDs. It is happily awarded the Dove "Family-Approved" Seal.*

CPSIA information can be obtained
at www.ICGtesting.com
Printed in the USA
LVHW070750160820
663144LV00032BA/405